BIMBO WINE OMNIBUS

SADIE THATCHER

1

CHEERS

Rebecca rang the bell. She heard the party inside already in full swing. New Year's Eve was not her kind of party, but she had agreed to make an appearance in a moment of weakness.

"You're here," Mark said when he opened the door to find his friend standing on the stoop. "Welcome, Rebecca. Please, come in."

However, before Rebecca could say or do anything, she suddenly became aware of one important fact. She was woefully underdressed for the party. Mark wore a tuxedo, going all out for the occasion. Behind him, inside the house, there were men dressed similarly. The women were all dressed in beautiful dresses, many of them little and black.

In comparison, Rebecca wore a frumpy red sweater, a pair of dark jeans, and retro styled trainers. Her plain brown hair was up in a basic ponytail. She did not even wear any makeup.

"Um," Rebecca said as she stepped inside, fully realizing the mistake. She did not even own an appropriate dress for a night like this.

"Don't worry about it," Mark said. "It's my fault for not clueing you in to the dress code for the party. I plum forgot about it when I invited you. But come in, get a drink, and mingle. There's still an hour before midnight."

Rebecca forced a smile as she headed toward the drinks table. If she was going to survive this, she needed booze to get through it.

Mark appeared for a second time, slipping behind the drinks table as if he were the bartender. "What can I get for you, ma'am," he asked professionally.

Rebecca laughed, appreciating the moment of levity. "So you're the host, the doorman, and the bartender now?"

"As the host, I can do whatever I want. And since it's my fault you didn't get the memo, I feel responsible for making the rest of your night as good as I can."

Rebecca looked over the drinks available. Usually she was not much of a drinker. When she did drink, it was usually wine out of a can, because she never drank two nights in a row. There were a lot of bottles on the table and Rebecca did not even know where to begin.

"How about a glass of champagne?" Mark suggested.

Rebecca nodded, accepting the offer. She figured that champagne was the way to go in any social setting. It classed her up a bit.

"Normally, I'd break this out closer to midnight, but this bottle was a gift from my friend for Christmas and not a part of the stock I originally planned to serve," Mark explained as he opened the bottle. The label was obscured and Rebecca could not see what was printed on it. Not that she knew anything about champagne. "He told me to share it with someone special and I think you count. This is definitely a special occasion."

"Thank you," Rebecca said as she took the offered glass.

"Cheers," Mark said, raising a glass of whatever he had been drinking prior.

"Cheers." They clinked their glasses together before Rebecca took her first delicious sip.

"So how's work?" Mark asked, making small talk. He knew the rest of his guests could enjoy themselves well enough. He felt responsible for Rebecca, making sure that she had a good time.

Rebecca took a moment to think about her answer. Should she tell Mark the truth or should she lie about how much she hated her job? She was little more than an office drone, pushing paper across her desk.

"Work sucks," Rebecca admitted.

"Maybe a new opportunity will present itself in the new year."

Rebecca rolled her eyes. It seemed unlikely. "I'd give up my job in an instant if the right opportunity came along. I'd love to be able to travel or really do anything exciting with my life."

Mark laughed. His eyes lit up when he saw his friend's enthusiasm. Rebecca had told him before about how bad things were at work, but the idea of being able to leave it all behind and pursue a more exciting career seemed to really resonate with him.

"I bet you have the perfect body to try your hand in modeling," Mark said as he refilled her champagne glass.

At the mention of the word modeling, Rebecca stopped mid-sip. She tried to remember if she had ever told him about her dream when she was younger. She actually wanted that once. But then her body developed the way it did and she realized she was far too shy to ever consider modeling. She hated being photographed now.

"In a different reality, perhaps," Rebecca said before she

resumed drinking. She did not know what else to say, because this was never a topic of discussion between the two of them.

But Mark did not let the comment pass him by. He kept talking and Rebecca kept drinking as he continued to make her feel comfortable at the party.

"The last of the bottle," Mark said as he tipped the last of the champagne into Rebecca's glass.

Rebecca drunkenly giggled. She could not remember the last time she drank so much. She was drinking a whole bottle. Rebecca had never done that before.

"Cheers," Mark said, holding out his cocktail glass.

"Cheers," Rebecca slurred before she downed the entire glass in one go.

"Whoa, someone's having a good night all of a sudden. That champagne looks like it went down easy. Maybe as the bartender I should be cutting you off tonight, huh?" Mark teased.

"What are you talking about?" Rebecca mumbled through a drink fog. "I'm not as think as you drunk I am."

Mark did not know what to say after that. But the pause gave Rebecca time to process her words. She started laughing. "I guess I am pretty drunk."

Mark laughed, too. He actually thought Rebecca was pretty cool and it was great to see her lighten up and enjoy herself. If she was not drunk, he would definitely be asking her out. But that would have to wait for her to be more sober.

Suddenly the crowd started counting. Midnight was almost here. Rebecca got a strange look in her eyes. They glistened with lust before she pulled him in for a kiss. Mark was stunned for a moment, but there was no way he It's was turning down a kiss from Rebecca. He kissed her back, returning her passion as his guests continued the countdown to midnight.

But the moment they all shouted "Happy New Year", something very different happened. Pink and sparkly magic wrapped around the kissing couple. Rebecca's eyes remained closed, but Mark had his open and he could only watch as he found himself frozen, unable to move or break the kiss.

He could see little from his position, but he watched as Rebecca's hair released itself from her ponytail and flowed down her back in loose waves. That was quickly followed by a bleaching of her hair, platinum blonde color leaching out from her roots and traveling out to the tips of her now much more voluminous hair. She looked like an entirely different person now with her light blonde locks falling down toward her ass.

However, that was not all that changed. Mark was only aware of a small portion of it as Rebecca's outfit transformed. Her red sweater lightened in color until it was a bright pink. It lengthened, the hem falling to just below her butt as it tightened on her thinning frame. The back of the dress then fell away, the neckline from the back dropping lower and lower until the small of her back was visible at the bottom. This was not a dress she was wearing a bra or panties with.

Rebecca's jeans moved down her body, melding with her shoes until they formed denim boots that wrapped around her lower legs, reaching to just below her knees. The material then turned pink, a similar color to her dress. Mark did notice how he suddenly did not need to lean over as far to maintain the kiss, Rebecca's shoes turning into tall stiletto-heeled boots.

Her outfit now clung to her modelesque figure, but she still lacked the necessary curves for her future life. This new

Rebecca was beautiful, but the magic would not finish until she was truly stunning.

It started with her breasts. Rebecca had never been big, but that was about to change. They started to balloon outward, becoming nearly as large as her head before they were finally stopped by Mark's body. Her nipples hardened with the new contact, the hard peaks standing out straight from her newly enlarged tits.

The dress stretched around Rebecca's tits, providing a substantial view of side boob. There was no way to believe her tits were natural. They stood off her chest, like they were bolted on, round and always prominent.

But there was no way that Rebecca could be left so top heavy without some additional modifications. Rebecca's ass started to bubble out from behind her, further stretching the sweater dress and forcing it to accommodate her extra curves. Its size did not quite match her expanded tits, but it was still impressive, always to leave people wondering if her cheeks were stuffed with plastic or if she was all natural below the waist. And to complete the picture, her ass grew until there was just a hint of cleavage on her backside, making it clear she wore nothing beneath the dress.

It was an impressive transformation, but the magic still swarmed around Rebecca and Mark. Her transformation was not yet complete. Heavy makeup bloomed across her face as her nose skimmed and her lips turned into plump cockpads. Pink remained a theme with her lipstick, lip gloss, and eye shadow.

That pink theme continued, too, as her fingernails lengthened and were painted pink. So were her toenails, but those were hidden by her boots.

Finally, however, the pink was broken as jewelry appeared on Rebecca's body. Gold hoop earrings appeared in her ears, large enough to almost reach her shoulders. Gold bangles appeared on her wrists. And a gold chain wrapped around her belly, threaded through her belly-button ring, but only visible from behind.

When Rebecca's physical transformation was finally complete, the sparkly pink magic absorbed into her head, giving her mind a boost to better match her new body.

When the pair were finally freed from their fixed embrace, Mark watched as his partner's eyes fluttered open. They immediately went wide when they took in Rebecca's new appearance. Her mouth opened, but she could not speak as it was stuck with a full set of fake lips, puffy and red. They stretched out across her entire face, creating an impossibly sexy pout that would have been perfect for a glamor shot.

"What happened?" she asked, her voice higher pitched, but with a lisp caused by the giant pout of her newly augmented lips. She could not believe her appearance had changed so drastically. "I... I feel different."

"Are you okay, Rebecca?" Mark asked, his expression a mix of concern and lust. Every change he saw in her, the tits, the lips, the slutty pink sweater dress, made his cock hard.

"Rebecca?" she said with a giggle. "Call me Bekki. That's totally a sexy name for a bimbo like me. I am going to start living up to my name today. Are you going to help me, or are you just going to watch?"

The change was complete and Bekki had already forgotten all about Rebecca. This new version of Rebecca had nothing in common with the woman she had been before. Her thoughts, the few she now had flitting around inside her head, were completely focused on fashion and sex. Her whole body had been redesigned with that in mind. But Bekki was clearly in heat, horny and ready to play.

"Let's get upstairs, baby," Bekki said, reaching for his hand, hoping he would lead her away from the crowd.

Mark did not need telling twice. He took Bekki's offered

hand and led her toward the stairs, pushing her along in front of him. That way he could watch the sexy sway of her hips, the way her bubble butt swung back and forth with each step.

He took the lead when they reached the stairs. All thoughts of his other guests were forgotten as he hurried up so he could watch Bekki ascend behind him, her bountiful bosom bouncing in the tight confines of her sweater dress. His cock had never been so hard.

Bekki giggled as she climbed the steps, enjoying how her body felt, so much more voluptuous than it had been before.

"You like my boobs?" she asked, looking up at Mark with lust-lidded eyes. Arousal coiled in her belly, making her pussy leak with anticipation. Even with how little she wore, a backless dress that barely covered her body, she still felt so hot, so ready to be fucked like a bimbo in heat.

"They're amazing," Mark said with a smile as he reached the top step. His eyes were glued to her sexy form, loving the impressive curves as they shifted from her big tits, tapering to her narrow waist, and then widening to accommodate her hips and ass. She had a perfect hourglass figure.

"What about my ass?" Bekki asked. "You want some of this, too?"

She turned around to present her butt. Her dress pulled tight against her ass, unable to completely cover her swollen cheeks. She was under constant threat to expose her bare slit, her lower lips glistening with her need.

"Yes," Mark said with a lusty grunt. He knew that she wanted to feel his cock in her mouth and between her tits, but his mind was more focused on her pussy. Bekki's tight snatch begged for attention. And if he was lucky, he would be able to give it all to her after she had taken a good pounding from his rock-hard erection.

Mark took hold of Bekki's hand again and practically

dragged her to his bedroom. Once the door was shut behind them, the sounds of the ongoing party below lowered to a muffle. He ordered the speaker to play the same music that was already playing downstairs, allowing the both of them to enjoy the party in a more private setting.

"How do you want me?" Bekki asked as she raised her hands together in the air, posing for Mark with a bent knee. Her dress strained against her body, her nipples almost escaping the sides of her dress, more of her tits becoming visible. The pink sweater dress appeared stretched to its limit, as if it could rip apart at any moment.

"That depends." Mark said with a smirk as he walked over to her. Bekki giggled, but remained still when she realized Mark intended to touch her. He moved behind her and ran his hands across her back.

Bekki sighed with pleasure when he touched her skin. It was always sensitive to his touch. His hands traveled around to her front and underneath the front of her dress, finally coming to rest on her augmented tits, his fingers pinching her hard nipples. Bekki moaned softly when she felt his fingers tugging at her hardened tips. She had never been so horny before.

"Oh God," Bekki groaned as she leaned back against Mark, pressing her ass into his already bulging crotch. "I want you."

"Then what are we waiting for?" Mark asked. He released her tits and lowered his hands to the hem of her tight sweater dress. He slid it up over her hips, removing what modesty she had left. Soon he had pulled it all the way up, pulling it over her head, leaving her body nude except for her pink denim boots.

She reached down to remove them, but Mark stopped her, grabbing her hands and placing them by her sides.

"No," he said. "Keep them on."

Bekki giggled as she lustily fluttered her long lashes at him, excited for all the fun they were about to have. She dropped gracefully to her knees and reached up to free Mark's straining cock. Her mouth watered at the prospect of sucking his shaft, the first step toward fulfilling her wildest desires.

She pulled Mark's member towards her face and wrapped her soft lips around his cock, gently suckling him, making sure he was completely hard for her.

"Yes," Mark groaned as the first waves of pleasure hit him. "You're such a fucking hottie! Suck that cock for me! I want to see that slutty look on your face as you take all of my cock."

"Mmmhmmm," Bekki hummed, bobbing her head in a sensual rhythm. One hand held his cock at the base, making sure every inch of him was pleasured, while the other dipped into her honeypot, driving her own arousal ever higher.

"Take me all the way," Mark commanded as his hands moved to remove his coat and shirt. "Deep throat my cock."

Bekki did not need telling twice. She took him to the root and then pulled back, gasping as she gulped in air. Her eyes watered, but her gaze remained fixed on his cock, a lusty grin spread across her pretty face before she dove back onto him again.

She continued this motion, sucking and slurping on Mark's member, enjoying the feel of his flesh sliding past her slick tongue, coating it with pre-cum as it slipped down her throat. The pleasure of the act was intense. The sensation of his cock hitting the back of her mouth made her head spin. It felt too good. Too right. And the way his big balls slapped against her chin made her moan out loud.

"I am going to cum, Bekki," Mark warned. She pulled away from him, leaving just the head inside her mouth. She used both hands to jack him off, using her saliva and her own juices as lubricant.

"Fuck, you look so fucking sexy when you blow me," Mark moaned. "So hot with my cock in your mouth. Now here it comes."

Mark unloaded in Bekki's mouth, his cock surging with his seed and sending rope after rope of his hot, white cum into her waiting mouth. Bekki swallowed eagerly, desperate to clean every drop up, to show him how much she wanted him.

Mark fell backwards, collapsing onto his bed, gasping for air as his climax ebbed. Bekki crawled up to lie beside him, taking his softening cock in her hand and slowly working him, pushing him to get hard all over again. Mark had cum and she had been given a tasty treat to chase all that champagne down, but she was not done yet. There was so much more fun to be had.

The two made love all night, Bekki begging and pleading for Mark to give her what she wanted, more orgasms. She took them all, giving as well as receiving, her mind completely lost in the pleasure, so much so that even when Mark came inside her, she kept begging him for more. She was insatiable, but Mark was more than up to the task of satisfying the horny bimbo.

"I am going to fill you up so good, baby," Mark said to her, kissing her tenderly on the lips. His words turned her on. He had never used those endearments with her before. But before tonight, they had merely been friends. Now that Rebecca had transformed into Bekki, there was so much more they could do together. They could be lovers. It was a new feeling for Bekki, but one that she enjoyed immensely.

Bekki moaned, running her hands down Mark's chest and stomach as he kissed her again. His fingers slid over her ass, his palms rubbing against her soft cheeks as she ground herself into him.

"Are you ready to go again?" Mark asked.

Bekki groaned lustily. She was always ready for more sex, but right now she would take whatever Mark offered. She didn't care what it was as long as she could satisfy her sexual appetite.

She nodded, eager for more, her lips locking on to Marks as their bodies continued to move in a sensual dance, his cock sliding between her tight lower lips. Her hips pushed up to meet his, the movement helping to drive his length deeper inside of her, until finally he bottomed out.

It was only moments later when Mark felt the pressure building up inside of him. He could feel the tingling rush of pleasure creeping along his shaft, signaling that he was close. He leaned forward and pressed his face into the crook of her neck, moaning softly, as he continued thrusting into her tight pussy.

Bekki moaned louder, her hands reaching down to wrap around Mark's strong thighs. She dug her nails into his skin, desperate to pull him into her as deeply as she could. And as Mark came inside of her, she let out a cry of delight, her body convulsing and quivering as another orgasm rippled through her.

"When do we stop? Mark asked. He had lost count of his orgasms on the night. He had lost count of the time.

Bekki shook her head, looking up at him with wide-eyed excitement. "Don't stop," she said as she looked down at his member and then back at his eyes. "Please keep going."

Mark could feel himself growing again. He didn't want this night to end. But even as he was about to come once more, he wanted to make it last for both of them. He leaned up and kissed Bekki on the lips, gently caressing her cheek as his fingers ran over her smooth skin. His eyes moved down to her tits, and he bent down to take one into his mouth. He sucked and licked all over her large breast, tasting their combined juices from when he had fucked her tits and enjoying her moans of pleasure.

"Oh yes," Bekki mewed, running her hands through his hair. She loved that Mark was such an impressive lover, with stamina and a willingness to taste her body. The feeling of having his hot tongue on her sensitive skin never grew old.

Mark pulled his head away, releasing her breast before he turned to the other one and repeated the actions, making sure he gave her nipples equal treatment. Bekki moaned out loud.

He reached down and lifted Bekki into his arms. She giggled as she felt the powerful muscles in his arm flex as he held her tight against his chest.

"How do you want me now?" Bekki asked, amazed that they were both still going.

Mark appeared pensive for a moment, carefully considering the situation. He felt so lucky to have been blessed with a woman like Bekki, who was willing to try new things, who was always up for sex, regardless of what time of night or day it was. And yet, here he was, wondering how to make this evening even better.

"I want your ass." It was the last part of herself that she could give him. He had cum in her mouth, on her tits, and multiple times in her pussy, but it was time to complete the package, becoming a perfect bimbo slut.

Bekki giggled at the thought, eager to take Mark's cock into her back door. She loved being a submissive bimbo whore, a sexual creature that had no qualms about being dominated. There was something about letting go that was so liberating.

Mark grabbed Bekki's hips and flipped her over, pulling her ass up so that she was on her hands and knees. He pushed his fingers into her pussy, scooping out her arousal. He then liberally coated her tight ass, preparing her for his cock.

"Do you want my cock in your ass?" Mark asked, giving her one last chance to back out, even though he already knew what her answer would be.

"Yes!" Bekki gasped.

"Then prepare yourself for me," Mark commanded. "You are going to love how I make you feel."

Bekki did not need telling twice. She relaxed her ass as Mark threaded his cock into her hole. She gasped as she was hit with a moment of pain, but that was quickly pushed away by the pleasure.

"Yes, yes! Oh God yes!" Bekki moaned as Mark slowly thrust in and out of her rear entrance. It felt amazing to have this gorgeous hunk of manhood deep inside her. Her tightness only enhanced the experience for both of them, his balls slap against her pussy with every powerful stroke.

"God you're tight, Bekki," Mark groaned.

Bekki giggled. This was just how she wanted it. She had turned into a sexual plaything for Mark and any other man who would have her. And right now she was more than willing to fuck any guy who took her for what she was worth. A perfect bimbo slut.

"You like my cock?" Mark asked, leaning over Bekki so that she could kiss him. She turned her head back and met his lips with hers, their tongues intertwining. They shared a long, hot, wet kiss, Mark's hands roaming up and down Bekki's body.

The kiss broke as Bekki moaned out loud, pushing her ass back towards Mark, making sure that he did not get distracted from fucking her. Her body shook with pleasure as Mark continued driving himself deep into her.

"So good, baby. So fucking good," Bekki moaned.

She was not the only one. The pleasure Mark was giving her was intense. He felt as though his dick might split in two from how tight she was squeezing his shaft. But he loved the feeling, reveling in every inch of her. There was no way he could ever be bored with her.

"Do you like my cock? Does it feel good inside of your pretty little ass?" he asked as he pulled away from their kiss to stare at her gorgeous face.

"Yes!" Bekki gasped. She had never been fucked in the ass before this evening but now that Mark was doing it, she knew it would quickly become one of her favorite things. His fingers were already sliding between her wet folds, teasing her clit as he worked her rear entrance.

"How does that feel? Are you enjoying yourself?" Mark asked, continuing to thrust in and out of her tight hole.

Bekki let out a long moan of delight. "So much," she moaned.

"Good. I want you to cum when I do. I want you to orgasm when you feel me fill your bowels with my cum."

It didn't take long for that to happen. As Mark kept fucking her ass, Bekki's whole body began shaking violently with pleasure, the orgasm fast approaching.

"Oh yes!" Bekki cried out as she neared her climax. She almost went over too soon, but then Mark came, blasting her insides with another load of his hot, white seed.

A powerful wave of orgasms crashed over her, one after the other. Her back arched up, pushing herself deeper into Mark, her eyes wide open in amazement.

"Thank you," she whispered in a soft voice. "That was amazing."

Mark smiled down at Bekki, running his hands across her smooth stomach as she relaxed again, lying on her back. This had been one of the most intense orgasms he had ever experienced. It was something else to have his cock inside such a tight place.

And he knew Bekki felt the same way. Her chest heaved with each breath, sucking in loads of air as she recovered from the exertion and pleasure of their multiple couplings. She was finally spent.

But he couldn't deny that he loved the feel of Bekki's soft body under him, her skin like satin against his. He never wanted this night to end.

However, end it must. After the pair finally caught their breaths, they decided it was time to check on the party downstairs. Was it even still going? Had the guests left or had they all passed out after a night full of revelry?

Rather than dress themselves, the pair pulled sheets and blankets off the bed and wrapped themselves in them for the trip downstairs. The white sheet Bekki chose was thin, barely hiding her still hard nipples. She held the sheet to her chest, not worrying about covering her ass. She had no shame in showing off her sexy figure to any adults.

They descended the stairs hand in hand, careful not to trip on the trailing bedding. Downstairs, the music was still going, but the party seemed to have reached a climax. Half the guests had left. Of the those remaining, half had passed out and the rest seemed to be in some state of undress, taking part in variations of what Mark and Bekki had been doing since midnight.

"Never mind us," Mark said. Keep doing what you're doing. We just need a little more booze before we go for round two."

Both Bekki and Mark had no idea what lay in store for them. It seemed unlikely that Bekki would be returning to work in the new year, but if he could manage to keep her around, Mark fully intended to put a ring on her finger as soon as possible. After tasting what a real bimbo slut could do, there was no going back for Mark.

As for Bekki, she was happy to go with the flow. Mark was a good friend and great fuck. Her mind had been stripped of those things that made her a good office worker. But where the champagne made by Bimbo Wine had taken away, it had given so much back in return. Bekki was supremely happy with her new life and she knew it would only get better from here.

2

HAPPY HOUR

"It looks like it's just us for happy hour today," Paul said after checking his phone.

"Carla and James can't make it again?" Bethany asked as the pair stood outside the bar.

Paul shrugged. "I guess I shouldn't have expected much different. Carla works too many hours now with her new job. It seems every time there's something fun going on, she has to work late."

"And James won't go anywhere without her," Bethany added.

Their happy hour group used to also include Mark, but ever since he had hooked up with Bekki at his New Year's Eve party, he had been too busy fucking her to be sociable as he used to be.

The two walked inside together, looking around. A few tables were occupied by people chatting about their days. One group had a TV playing sports highlights.

"Is there a preference for where you want to sit?" Paul asked.

Bethany nodded toward one table near the back corner.

The seats faced away from most of the crowd, giving them some privacy.

Paul sat down first before pulling out Bethany's chair. She smiled, glad he was being polite. As she sat, she pushed her brown hair behind her ears, keeping it away from her face. Her hands felt clammy as she picked up the happy hour menu on the table. She did not want to reveal her true feelings for Paul, afraid of what he would say if she expressed them.

Paul sat across from her at the small table. It was an intimate setting, with a candle on the table. This could have been a date, if they were both honest about their feelings. Bethany had a crush on Paul, but he had feelings for Bethany, too. Although his desires would have made a relationship difficult, even if they were both honest with each other.

"What do you recommend?" Paul asked.

"You know me, I'm a red wine girl," Bethany replied. She scanned the wine list, but made a face at the number of white wines on the menu. Her choices were limited.

"I'll be drinking beer," Paul said. It was an indication of their divergent interests, making it difficult to find common ground, despite their affections for each other. "See anything you like?"

Bethany scanned a wine list for a second time. There were three reds on the list, but she'd already had two of them before. Bethany liked the variety of trying different wines. That left one option, a red blend from a winery called Bimbo. She shook her head. That had to be a typo.

However, before Bethany could think about it too much, the waiter appeared. "I'm Roger. Can I get you started on drinks today?" He was a bit brusk, but both Paul and Bethany assumed he was at the end of a long shift and tired. If he'd been working since lunch, they knew they would be, too.

"The red blend for me," Bethany said. She did not want to

say the name of the winery, finding it weird. And if it was a typo, she did not want to be the one to call attention to it. Usually Bethany was full of confidence, but there was something about being around Paul that made her nervous.

"And I'll have the kölsch," Paul added.

Roger wrote down their orders and snapped his little book shut. "I'll be right out with those. And if you want to order food, I'll check in with you soon."

And with that, the pair were alone again. Bethany played with the he, of her sweater, not sure what to say. Paul reached across the table to grab her hand, and Bethany jumped, not expecting his touch The two stared into each other's eyes, unsure of what to do next.

"So… you had a good day?" Paul asked.

"Yes. It was busy." Bethany was not sure what else she could tell him. Work was complicated and she was coming to the end of her contract. She had no idea what she would do next. It was something else she was nervous about.

Paul smiled and squeezed Bethany's hand. They were quiet for a moment before Bethany spoke again.

"What about you?" Bethany asked.

"It went well, too. My boss was in a great mood, and told me I might be up for a promotion soon."

"That would be nice!" Bethany agreed.

The two chatted a bit more, sharing work stories before another waiter brought them their drinks. Roger was nowhere to be seen. Paul's came in a pint glass, but Bethany's wine seemed to fill an entire wine glass. It was a lot.

"Wow, that's a lot of wine," Paul commented. Bethany's eyes were big, staring at the large glass. Her heart started to race as she picked it up. A sense of worry filled her body. Could she drink all of this? At least she did not need to drive home.

Bethany took a sip from her glass, wincing slightly at the

sweet taste. It certainly wasn't her preferred wine, but that would not stop her from drinking it.

"Not what you thought it would be?" Paul asked.

"I didn't think this would be so sweet," Bethany replied. "It's almost like they added sugar syrup to it."

However, rather than set the glass back down, Bethany took another sip. And then another.

"Looks like it's growing on you," Paul said before he took a drink from his own glass. This was a beer he knew well and enjoyed. Paul generally knew what he liked and why, which made his interest in Bethany all the more strange. She was not his usual type.

"Yes. Yes it is," Bethany said, taking another sip. The red wine continued to take effect as she relaxed more and more. And the conversation started to get away from her, too. She was barely aware of what they were talking about. However, Bethany could not help but smile at the handsome Paul, a heat growing between her legs.

"Are you okay?" Paul asked, suddenly concerned by the sudden color in her cheeks. He had never seen Bethany react this way to alcohol before. And he had seen her drunk. This was something else.

"Yes, yes I am," Bethany replied. She took another sip to reassure him. The alcohol was taking hold as she talked to Paul, making her more open to him. Now it was her reaching out and holding his hand. Neither of them noticed as her once professionally short nails grew out to a glamor length and turned pink.

Paul looked down at their hands, seeing her fingernails, not remembering them being like that before, but his cock got hard at the idea of what those fingers could do for him. He shifted in his seat, trying to give his growing hardness more room in his pants.

"I hope I can drink this much," Bethany said. Her eyes

were half closed, as if the alcohol was giving her some sort of drug-induced stupor. And yet, she felt great. That was the weird part. She felt a little drunk, but she also felt alive in a way she never had before.

When Bethany opened her eyes fully again, they were framed with long, thick lashes, highlighting her suddenly blue eyes.

Paul had to do a double take as he looked into her eyes. There was something happening here that did not make sense. But rather than blame the Bimbo Wine, he looked down at his beer, wondering if he had been drugged and was now hallucinating.

However, there was no mistaking Bethany. Her features had changed. Her face had become more feminine, her cheekbones higher. And those full, lush lips looked far better suited to sucking on a dick, especially the way they were swathed in pink lipstick.

"Wow, Bethany. You look incredible!" Paul exclaimed, staring at his friend as if she were someone completely different. He couldn't help it. It was all he could think about as his cock throbbed in his pants, demanding attention.

A giggle escaped Bethany's lips in response to the compliment. She never giggled before, but now giggles erupted from her with comfortable ease. "Mmm," she purred, her voice taking on a higher pitched tone, but holding a huskiness that highlighted her own arousal.

There were other changes happening to Bethany as she sat there, but the table and her bulky sweater hid much of them from Paul's view. Her ass expanded in her pants, straining the previously loose fabric to its breaking point. Her hips widened to match, making sure she always had something to sway as she walked.

Bethany's waist narrowed, her midriff tightening. Her organs shifted as her body morphed, making room to give her an exaggerated hourglass figure that men would go crazy over.

It was Bethany's breasts that would ultimately become her most notable feature. They took on a clearly augmented look, becoming rounded and almost bolted onto her chest. Her bra completely dissolved, making it easy for her to grow without noticing it. But even as her breasts slowly grew bigger and bigger, they were not what Paul noticed on his friend.

The changes he witnessed came together. Bethany's skin smoothed, her freckles disappearing as she gained a golden tan. And while Paul could not see her skin everywhere, it was a tan that was even all over her body, even where her body hair had once grown.

And simultaneously, Bethany's brown hair began to fade in color as it grew down her back. By the time it reached her butt, it was platinum blonde. Her roots were the same color, indicating that this was the color it would grow from now on.

Paul still assumed he was hallucinating, but he drank down his beer, loving the image he saw in front of him. Bethany was truly beautiful in his eyes now. She was everything he could have ever wished for in a potential partner. And the way she seemed to be looking at him made him want her all the more.

But it only got better as Bethany's breasts grew into a proper pair of tits, stretching out her sweater. She reached up and jiggled her tits in her top, trying to find more space for them. It was an unconscious action, one that looked practiced from years of having tits like that.

Bethany giggled, not quite able to hide it anymore. A soft moan escaped her lips as she watched Paul. She could see him staring at her as he sat there in disbelief. And the look in his eyes sent a thrill through her stomach. Maybe he wanted her as much as she wanted him.

However, before Bethany could make her move on Paul, her clothing began to shift and change. Her dark sweater lightened in color as it became thinner. The neckline lowered, showing off her new cleavage. The valley her top now put on display was long and deep, drawing in every male eye into its depths, even Paul's

Bethany's top turned a bright pink, matching her lips and nails. The hem also rose up and it hugged her body, stopping just above her belly-button, revealing a dangling piece of jewelry with several pink jewels that reflected the light wonderfully.

Bethany's new body was a sight to behold, but there were still a few additional changes that needed to be made before she was complete. Her pants slid up her legs and turned into a tight skirt that hugged her hips and ass, barely reaching the tops of her thighs. The straps of her pink thong reached up over the top of the navy blue skirt, creating further contrast in colors and giving everyone an idea of what her new body was designed for.

When Bethany stepped into the bar, she did so wearing dark canvas shoes. The darkness remained, the color shifting to a navy blue to match her skirt, but the style of shoe changed radically. They transformed into stiletto pumps with a heel that Bethany could never have imagined walking in because they were so high, complete with red soles.

With the physical transformations complete, Bethany looked down into her deep cleavage and a moment of lucidity returned to her.

"Something's wrong," she said. But her voice was different now. It was much higher than before and husky. And the way it sounded was somehow familiar, although she could not explain why. She reached up to smooth out her hair, finding it longer and straighter.

Panic began to build in Bethany's chest, but she felt the calming influence of her new body, running her fingers through her long hair, touching the sides of her tits, emphasizing her incredible cleavage.

Bethany looked down into her empty glass. There was just a tinge of pink left, the last drop of red wine reflecting the light.

"I'm drunk," Bethany announced as she looked up into Paul's eyes, meeting his gaze. She sensed how aroused he was, although it was clear he was not listening to her words. He was still under the impression that he was hallucinating.

A new sense of calm overcame Bethany at her realization. If she was drunk, it just meant that her eyes were deceiving her. She did not have huge, fake tits. She did not have long, blonde hair. She did not look like a bimbo.

But before Bethany could further think on her situation, the final bits of magic from her drink entered her mind. It left her memories of the past intact, but it made them difficult to access. The connections in her mind that made her smart and a capable employee were shifted, giving her an impressive understanding of all things fashion and sex. Those were going to be her new hobbies from now on.

And the final change came in the form of her name. Bethany still technically existed, but she was hidden beneath so many layers of a new bimbo personality that there was now only Beth.

Beth smiled at Paul, no longer finding anything wrong with her situation. If anything, it all felt right. She felt sexy and horny and she was finally going to hook up with the love of her life. Those feelings that Bethany had for Paul became stronger without her old inhibitions and worries.

Beth reached across the table and gently held Paul's

muscular arm. She licked her lips as she looked into his face with lust-lidded eyes. Beth could not remember ever being this aroused before. She felt like she was in heat, needing Paul to fuck her as soon as possible. Her nipples pressed hard against the thin material of her sweater, standing at attention, and they seemed to ache as she stared at the man she loved with all her heart.

Paul looked up from Beth's magnanimous tits and into her eyes. He smiled, his cock harder than he had ever experienced before.

"Bethany," Paul said, his voice cracking.

"Beth," she corrected him.

"Beth," he said, his voice still strained, but no longer cracking. "Do you want to—"

"Yes," Beth interrupted. She could not hold herself back.

Paul reached for his wallet, now suddenly hurried to get out of there. He pulled money from his wallet and tossed it on the table, certain that he was leaving enough money for their drinks and a hefty tip. He did not understand what had happened to the woman sitting before him, but he was not about to withhold his thanks.

Paul stood up and Beth pushed herself to her feet. He held out his hand to her, but when she took it, she pulled him close. Her tits pushed into his chest as she reached up and wrapped her arms behind his neck. Their lips met, her tongue darting into his mouth, forcing him to reciprocate.

He didn't know how she could kiss so passionately, but he was happy to return her passion. And he certainly wasn't going to stop it. His hands traveled down her back until they found her ass. He grabbed her cheeks and pulled her closer to him.

Beth spread her legs so that his thigh was pressing up against her panty-covered pussy, making her groan with pleasure into his mouth at the contact. She couldn't remember ever feeling this horny, this needy for some cock. It felt incredible.

Paul pulled away and looked her in the eyes. She looked up at him, her long lashes fluttering. She knew exactly what she wanted from him and she was going to have it.

"My place or yours?" Paul asked. Even though he had dreamed of having such a bimbo at his beck and call, he was still a gentleman and cared about what she wanted, no matter how simple her thoughts and feelings had become.

"Yours," Beth said, running her hands up and down his arms.

Paul took charge, grabbing Beth's hand and leading her out of the bar. His pace was fast enough she was almost tripping over herself as she tried to keep up with her bimbo body and sky high heels.

Beth moaned softly when they made it outside, her nipples responding to the cold night air. She had not worn a jacket, so she pressed her body into Paul's side as they walked toward his house. Her hips gyrated in time with their progress.

Paul reached up and pushed some stray hairs behind her ear, taking in the sight of her big boobs bouncing beneath her sweater as he did. He could see she was wearing no bra under the sweater and her nipples were clearly visible, poking against the fabric. He had to get her home so he could fuck her, the faster the better.

They made terrific time. As soon as they were inside, Paul guided her to his bedroom, bypassing the kitchen and living rooms. They might visit those later, but for now, the bedroom was the best place for them to fuck.

Paul pushed Beth down on his bed and she fell with a soft thump and a moan of delight. Her legs wrapped around his waist and she tugged his shirt open, allowing her hands to explore his chest and abs. She kissed him eagerly as she did so, pushing her tongue into his mouth, forcing him to respond with his own eagerness.

Paul pulled off his belt and undid his pants, shoving them down as well, letting his huge, fat cock spring free. Beth looked at the massive weapon in awe, never having seen such a large erection before.

"You like that?" Paul asked, his voice hoarse as he pawed at Beth's tits.

Beth moaned, her eyes closing, as she tried to imagine how it would feel inside her pussy. But she needed to taste that big cock first.

Paul grabbed Beth by the hips, pulling her off the bed as he knelt over her, guiding his big dick toward her face.

She opened wide, taking him deep into her mouth and sucking on it, enjoying the taste of him, savoring his thick rod.

"Ahh, Beth, that feels so good," Paul groaned as she bobbed up and down on his shaft, licking all over the head while she sucked in earnest.

She looked up at Paul, seeing his big blue eyes looking back at her, staring down with love and lust. He looked amazing with a raging hard-on. His cock was long and thick and she loved wrapping her cock pads around it, her lips being designed for just this purpose.

"Beth," Paul groaned, his hands running through her hair, guiding her movements ever so slightly, encouraging her to take him deeper and deeper into her throat.

It was almost too much for her to handle and she gagged, trying to pull back. Her body trembled and she felt like she might vomit, but she did not want to stop. She wanted him deep in her throat. She wanted him to fill her mouth with his hot cum and watch the pleasure on his face as he climaxed.

Her body convulsed, shaking as she struggled to hold back. She did not want to let go of his cock. She loved feeling it slide past her tongue and down her throat, trying to take it all. Beth was in ecstasy, her mind lost to pleasure, nothing else important at the moment. She didn't even feel like she existed, that she could think about anything other than how good it felt.

"Beth!" Paul called out to her.

Beth looked up, his voice coming out of nowhere, causing her to startle.

"I'm going to cum."

Beth pulled back so that just the head of his cock was in her mouth. She reached up with her long-nailed fingers and stroked his cock, jacking him off so he would spill his first load of seed directly into her mouth. She wanted, no needed, to taste him fully.

"Fuck yes," Paul called out as he came. His cum filled Beth's mouth as she kept sucking. But she did not swallow. She collected all his cum in her mouth, savoring the flavors that danced across her tongue.

"Wow," Paul gasped as Beth pulled her face back from his throbbing erection.

She opened her mouth, showing him his cum in her mouth. Then she closed her lips and made a big show of swallowing it down. When she opened wide again, it was all gone.

"Good girl," Paul said, patting her head.

Beth grinned. She liked getting rewarded for pleasing Paul. His cum was so delicious. She would happily suck him off anytime he wanted. Except, there was one thing she still needed. She needed him to fuck her.

"How soon can you go again?" Beth asked as she nuzzled her face against Paul's muscular thigh.

"For you, as soon as possible. Let me freshen up for a moment while you prepare yourself."

As soon as Paul was gone, Beth set to work, wanting to be

more than ready for his return. She pulled her sweater up and over her head. The moment her tits were free, they bounced on her chest, no longer confined by her tight top.

Beth giggled as her tits swung back and forth while she leaned over to push her skirt down. She stepped out of the miniskirt, keeping her heels on. All she wore now was her pink thong. It hugged her wet slit tightly as she stood before the full-length mirror. She turned this way and that, admiring her body. Her boobs, her ass, her pretty face, even her long eyelashes were just as amazing as Paul said.

But for Beth to truly prepare herself for Paul's return, even the sexy thong had to go. She slipped her long-nailed fingers beneath the straps and pushed them down past her hips and over her thighs. Her gaze never left the mirror as she performed a sexy dance to music only she could hear.

Once Beth found a home for her discarded clothing, she climbed onto the bed, still wearing her sexy high heels. She stretched her body, contorting it into the sexiest pose she could imagine. It was important that she highlight her body for Paul's return. She wanted the sight of her to make him hard again. She needed him so bad. She couldn't wait until he returned to the bedroom.

Beth felt like such a slut for wanting this cock so badly. But then, she didn't remember a time when she didn't want men to fuck her senseless. The time before her transformation was hazy and fragmented. All her old memories were technically still there, but they were hidden behind an almost impenetrable pink fog, a veil that she had no interest in piercing. It was so much easier to embrace being the dumb and sexy bimbo she had turned into.

Beth closed her eyes tight and imagined what it would feel like to be fucked by Paul once more. She let out a soft moan, imagining it happening. In the back of her mind she wondered how long this night could last, but at least she knew her wait for him would be short. Beth had half a mind to begin stroking her clit and pussy, edging herself while she waited for him. But the simple fact was Beth was already insanely horny. She did not need to touch herself to prepare for him. She was already on a razor thin edge, ready to be pushed over at any moment. And something told her she should wait for her first bimbo orgasm to come from Paul's cock and not her nimble fingers.

Paul stepped back into the bedroom, completely nude. He stood, feet shoulder width apart, his hands on his hips, standing like a superhero. His cock quickly rose to attention at the sight of the sexy bimbo posing on his bed.

"Are you ready for me to fuck you?" he asked as he sauntered closer to her.

Beth giggled at the idea, unable to resist flirting with him. She was more than ready. Her pussy throbbed with need, her whole body aching for his touch. She had never wanted anything more than to feel him inside her, filling her with his hard, fat cock.

"You already know the answer to that, big boy. I want you so bad."

She knew exactly what she wanted and how to get it. There was no other way this could end. She turned and spread her legs. Her parting thighs revealed her pussy, dripping with desire. Beth moaned, letting her head fall back against the headboard.

"Do it. Take me now. Fuck me!" Beth screamed out loud, not caring if anyone heard her or not. It was too late anyway. This was her life now, being a bimbo and nothing else. She wanted Paul to use her however he wanted and she knew she would love every second of it.

Paul climbed onto the bed, growing ever closer to her. Beth's were transfixed by his cock as it bobbed in time with the beating of his heart, every pulse of blood making him harder for her body.

But even as Paul brought his cock tantalizingly close to her pussy, teasing her with how he almost pushed the head into her, his eyes were fixated on hers. He leaned in for a kiss. They had shared dozens of these kisses, but never like this. Never before had Paul kissed her as though it might be their last one. She was sure there was no tomorrow.

They kissed for a long time, Paul using his tongue to playfully tease Beth's mouth, trying to work up her own saliva and get her more excited for what was to come. She couldn't stop herself from pressing her hips closer and closer to him, begging for contact, but he always kept his cock just out of reach. He was going to fuck her, but they would be on his terms.

"Please," Beth begged.

"What? What do you want, baby?" Paul asked as he pulled his lips back from her mouth. He smiled at her and then leaned in, kissing her once more.

"I need your cock. I need it now. I'm on fire. Please, fuck me."

Paul saw the madness of her lust forming in her eyes. He had always wanted to have a busty, blonde bimbo at his beck and call, but he now understood that such wonderful luck came with great responsibility. He needed to keep her well and truly fucked if he hoped to hold her love.

"Tell me who you love."

"I love you. I love your cock. Now hurry up and fuck me. Fuck your bimbo slut."

How could Paul say no to that? He positioned his cock at her entrance and pushed himself in.

Beth came immediately, her body shaking as her first bimbo orgasm hit her. The pleasure was greater than anything she had ever felt before, the orgasm so intense her whole world went black around her, replaced only by a white, blinding light. But this did not last long. She had barely time to come down when she found herself thrusting herself onto Paul, her hips rolling to meet his every thrust.

She knew she wasn't in control of herself right now. She was simply reacting to what was happening to her. She would do anything for that cock inside of her. Even beg him to keep fucking her. It was so easy to forget that she had been anything other than a stupid bimbo now. She had turned into this hot mess because it felt so good to have such a manly dick pounding her pussy. And the more Paul fucked her, the better she liked it.

Beth was beyond caring who or what she had become. All she cared about was Paul fucking her as hard and deep as he wanted, over and over again.

"Your pussy feels so fucking good," Paul groaned with pleasure.

It was all too much for Beth, too much for her to handle. She began to buck against Paul, wanting to feel his dick inside of her as fast and hard as possible. She wanted nothing more than to be used and fucked until she collapsed under Paul, completely spent and satisfied.

"Yes. Yes, fuck me. Harder. Make me cum."

"I think we both are going to cum tonight, baby. And even once we do, we're not done yet."

"Fuck yes. More. More fucking. More cumming. Fuck me with your big, hard cock."

Beth was delirious with the pleasure coursing through her body. But the only way it could get better was if Paul came inside her, filling her up with his hot load. The more Paul fucked her, the more she felt her juices dripping down her legs. Her pussy was aching for another orgasm. Her bimbofied mind was in agreement. It was all she wanted. She wanted to cum on Paul's thick shaft as he impaled her, splitting her open with every thrust.

Beth could not get enough of how he filled her, driving himself so deep inside of her that her eyes watered with pain and pleasure. She moaned out loud with pleasure, knowing that this was the best fucking she had ever experienced and knowing that it was only going to get better. Her hips moved instinctively, thrusting forward to meet his. The bed beneath them shook as he rode her like a wild man. This was a night of firsts for the both of them and Beth intended to make sure it was one to remember.

Beth screamed out loud. "Fucking cum inside me. I want your hot sperm all over me. Fill my belly up with your baby batter. I love having your dick inside me, so deep. So fucking good!"

And that was exactly what Paul did. He unleashed his cum, sending surge after surge of his thick cum inside of her. He let out an animalistic roar as he held himself inside of her.

But Beth was cumming, too. She screamed out as the pleasure overwhelmed her. Her vision turned white as the endorphin rush hit her head on, inundating her with every pleasurable hormone her body could produce. She came again and again as Paul's cock pulsed inside of her, leaving her exhausted.

A dopey smile formed on her face as she lay next to Paul, his softening cock slipping out of her wet pussy. Beth had just experienced the most intense sex of her life. And she looked like it. Her hair was messy, her makeup smeared, and her pussy leaked a combination of their fluids. She looked well and truly fucked.

"Holy fuck," Paul gasped as he breathed heavily, his chest rising and falling in time with Beth's. They were both exhausted and in need of recovery.

Beth giggled. She couldn't help herself. She had never felt like this before. But more importantly, she had never felt so happy. She knew this should not be real, but it was. And it felt amazing.

"When can we do it again?" Beth asked.

Paul stared at her, dumbfounded. She looked like she could barely keep her eyes open and she still wanted more. It seemed impossible, but Paul's cock was already making an attempt to rise again.

"Damn, woman, we're only human," Paul said, flabbergasted. But there was no way he could say no to such a deliciously hot and sexy bimbo. He was in love with Beth, more than ever. And she was in love with him. The rest they could figure out when the time came.

Beth giggled again. It was almost her default state. It said so much more than words could.

Paul wrapped his arm around Beth's shoulder. He reached down and played with her nipple. She kept giggling.

"I'll need some time, but we can go again soon enough."

Beth pressed herself into Paul's side, cuddling with him. She reached out and gently stroked his cock, aiding his recovery, without even thinking about it. But she would wait for him.

The pair laid there together, enjoying their shared heat. Neither of them knew what the future held, but they were both intent on making it work. Beth wanted nothing more than to continue as Paul's bimbo. She loved her new sexy body. She loved the way she made Paul's cock hard. And she loved the simplicity of her new life.

Beth never wanted to be a bimbo before, but now that she was one, she could not imagine a better life for herself. She was living a dream made real and it was all thanks to a glass of Bimbo Wine.

3

DATE NIGHT

"Good, Carla, you're here," James said as his girlfriend approached their table. He looked relieved. "I was starting to get worried you wouldn't make it."

"Sorry, I got held up at work." Carla sat down with a sigh. Her mind was less focused on James and more on the work she left behind at the office. She was still debating whether she should return to work after their date to get more work done. That was one reason she never bothered to change out of her work suit.

James took Carla's hand as they sat across from each other. "I'm glad you could make it. I've missed our date nights and evenings spent together." In comparison, James was dressed more casually, wearing khaki pants and a button-down shirt. She was all business and he was business casual, at best.

Carla tried to smile at him. "I do, too." Although she was not entirely truthful. Carla loved James. The problem was she loved her job more. Her recent promotion had her working insanely long hours. She often remained at the office late into the night. And she did not even have weekends to herself. The building security guards all knew her by face and name. She knew many of their names as well, just from their frequent interactions.

James leaned forward, hoping they might share a more intimate moment at their table before the waiter arrived, but she pulled away. They both sighed. They had been arguing about the amount of time they spent together, but Carla refused to spend less time at the office. If James did not know her better, he would have assumed she was cheating on him. But office romance was the last thing on Carla's mind. It would go against her ethics.

"We need to make the most of the time we do have together," James said as he picked up his menu.

Carla followed suit, perusing the wine list. Nothing stood out to her as amazing or something she was dying to try. There was even one wine made by a winery with bimbo in the name. Carla assumed that had to be a typo. That or bimbo meant something else in a foreign language. Maybe it was a family name.

The waiter arrived, putting pressure on Carla to make her wine choice. Her eyes kept returning to the Bimbo Wine. It was a Pinot Grigio, which was a little sweet for her usual tastes, but under pressure, she chose it.

James ordered a red wine after she pointed out her preference on the menu. Carla could not bring herself to call it Bimbo Wine. And just like that, Carla's future was set.

"I'll return momentarily with your drinks," the waiter said before he left the table to fulfill their order.

"I assume you're going to the office this weekend," James said with a note of sadness.

"Bright and early tomorrow," Carla answered. They both knew their Friday night date night would be a bust in the end. If Carla had an early morning scheduled, it meant it would be a sexless night. Even though the pair lived together and even slept in the same bed, it felt more and more like they were just roommates.

There was still love there, but Carla's job had driven a wedge between them. Their arguments over it had become increasingly frequent. But now their date night was probably ruined. Carla knew if she went back to the office, she would only end up staying later than she already had been. It was a compulsion, maybe even an addiction, to spend her free time working. She found herself incapable of shutting down her work life, letting it leak into her love life.

Understanding that talk of work was not getting him anywhere, James decided to shift the conversation. "Have you seen Bethany's social media posts this week?"

"You know I don't have time for social media," Carla countered, but her interest was piqued. "But what happened?"

"Apparently she dyed her hair blonde and got implants, or something. She's been posting all of these revealing selfies this week. Makes me wish I'd gone to happy hour with her and Paul last week. Maybe I'd know what was going on."

"That's so weird," Carla said. "And right after Mark started dating that bimbo, Bekki, too. Do you think it's related?"

"How could it be? People don't change that fast. This had to be a long time coming."

However, before the gossip could continue, the waiter returned with their drinks. "Are you ready to order food?"

It was only then that they both realized they hadn't considered the menus since they ordered their drinks. They had been too busy gossiping about their friends.

"I guess we need a moment," James said. However, they were once again faced with a distraction when a customer and bus boy, carrying a load of dirty dishes, collided. All those dishes went crashing to the floor, causing a major disturbance in the restaurant. The waiter rushed over to assist, leaving the unhappy couple on their own.

"Whoa, that's a big glass of wine," Carla said once she finally looked down at her delivered drink. The wine glass was nearly filled to the top. James had a normal pour.

"I guess you won't be needing a refill," James joked. "But hopefully it's good."

Carla picked up the heavy glass and took a tentative sip. Her eyes widened as the delicious flavors flowed over her tongue. She started to drink in earnest, almost chugging it until she had downed half of the glass.

"Easy there," James said.

"Sorry, I didn't mean to get carried away," Carla said. "It's really good."

James smiled. It was good to see her let loose for once. She could be so uptight.

Normally, Carla would have swirled the wine in her glass. She had learned to do that when she and James went wine tasting last year. That was before her promotion at work. She would have even tasted it as she had learned to do, but the moment the wine entered her mouth, such desires were overridden by the simple drive to drink more.

"Can I try a sip?" James asked, genuinely curious about this new wine.

But Carla immediately got a possessive look in her eyes. She clutched the glass in her hand and took another long drink.

James would have laughed if this was not such unusual behavior for his girlfriend. Instead, he felt himself needing to apologize to keep the peace. "It's okay. You don't need to share if you don't want to. I'm sorry, but I was just curious." James picked up his own glass and took a sip, enjoying his preferred red wine.

It only took minutes for Carla to finish her wine. She let out a satisfied sigh as she set the empty glass down.

"If that glass wasn't so big, I'd order you another," James said, but it quickly became clear that Carla was not listening. Her eyes glazed over, the brown lightening, turning blue.

James pinched himself, thinking he must be dreaming, but it was all real.

After the change in eye color, Carla's clothing started to change. The table blocked much of James' view, but her suit jacket melted away and the blouse beneath it melded with her pants. Those pants began to rise up her legs, merging together until it had turned into a dress. The whole thing looked strange at first, but it did not take long before it had transformed into a low-cut mini-dress.

But that was not all that changed. Carla's bra and her panties disappeared. Her small breasts were very much on display in the low-cut dress. Her legs were bare beneath the table as well.

And then the dress itself went through a final transformation, turning pink and covered in sparkly sequins. The dress glittered and shimmered in the light, attracting attention that Carla never would have been comfortable with before.

The dress hugged Carla's body. The stress from her job was already starting to add pounds to her waistline. Not that she was fat, but her once slim body had been lost. But it was lost no longer. The magic of the wine went to work, removing the excess fat, giving her a tight and toned body. Her legs and arms became svelte, looking delicate, but remaining strong. The dress shrunk with her body, maintaining its figure hugging qualities.

James stared on, not wanting to believe what he was seeing. This was impossible. How could any of this be happening?

"You look beautiful," James said when he finally gathered

the nerve to speak. However, Carla remained oblivious to what was happening, her eyes still glazed as the magic from her wine continued to work.

Carla's hair was next. Her plain brown hair lengthened and lightened as it grew out from her head. It only took moments before she sported voluminous, platinum blonde hair that fell in loose waves all the way down her back, almost reaching the seat of her chair.

A deep tan spread all over Carla's body, leaving behind perfectly even and hairless skin. There were no tan lines to be seen on her body. And the darker color somehow made Carla's small boobs look bigger, although it was only a matter of lighting.

If the magic had stopped there, James would have been more than excited. Left at home by his girlfriend more often than not, he had been left to take care of his own needs and seeing both Beth and Bekki on social media, showing off their bimbofied bodies, was more than enough masturbation fodder for him. Only now Carla had the same basic look, although without all the same attributes.

However, the magic was not done. Carla's face bloomed with heavy makeup as her eyelashes lengthened, her nose narrowed, and her lips inflated into plump pleasure pillows. With her glazed eyes, Clara now had the look of a dazed bimbo, at least when it came to her face. The rest of her body had yet to get the same treatment.

But where nature had been frugal, the Bimbo Win magic was generous. It started with her waist, further shrinking it, giving her a wasp-like middle that would always look like she wore a tight corset, even though she never did.

A good portion of the mass from Carla's middle moved to her ass, giving her a bubble butt that any bimbo would be proud of. Her ass bubbled up beneath her, raising her up off the chair and helping her to sit up straighter, pushing her small boobs out.

But those boobs were not small for long. They grew out from her chest, blowing up like two balloons. They got bigger and bigger until they were roughly on par in size with both Beth and Bekki. They were big and looked incredibly fake with the way they seemed almost bolted onto her chest.

James' eyes nearly bugged out as he saw Carla's new tits trying to burst free from her dress. And given how low her neckline dipped, it was clear there was no magic bra creating the illusion of such breathtaking cleavage. This was Carla's new reality.

However, with every physical change that had taken place, transforming Carla's body and outfit, there was yet one part of her that had remained untouched: her mind. But all things must end and the life of the workaholic Carla had reached its end.

The magic infused itself into Carla's brain, rewiring her neural pathways. The uptight personality that had caused so much friction with James melted away. In its place a new happy and horny personality formed. Where once she delighted in hard work, now she loved fashion and sex. Thinking became a chore that she preferred to ignore. She was a bimbo now, in body and mind.

When her eyelashes fluttered, the glazed look in her eyes getting replaced with happy confusion and lust, it was no longer Carla looking out through those eyes. It was Carli, the happiest of bimbos who was deeply in love with her boyfriend.

"Wow, Carla, you're so fucking hot," James said. He didn't care if his voice carried. He was too transfixed by his girlfriend's new body.

Carli giggled at the compliment. She loved giggling. It just felt so good and it sometimes made her big tits jiggle.

"Thanksies," she finally said, her voice both higher pitched and softer, perfect for her new bimbo look. There was also the tiniest hint of a lisp, her big lips getting in the way of normal speech patterns. "But you should, like, totes call me Carli. That's, like, such a better name and stuff for a bimbo like me."

"Right, Carli," James said, trying out the new name for the first time. He found himself liking it. He liked the name as much as he liked her new body.

"I'm, like, totally horny," Carli said. "I want your big cock so bad right now."

And it also seemed that Carli did not care where she was. She would happily talk about sex, no matter what situation she was in or who might be listening. It was dangerous, yet so hot.

"Waiter, check," James called out.

The waiter deposited the check in quick order, almost like he was expecting an early exit for the now happy couple. James paid quickly and then he took Carli by the hand and pulled her from the restaurant, unable to wait even an extra second to get home. His cock strained in his pants.

The drive home was fast. They had left Carli's car at the restaurant. They would have to return for it later. There was no way James was letting his girlfriend out of his sight until he fucked her, fully claiming her. They would find out tomorrow that her once sensible car had transformed into a hot pink convertible, the magic changing Carli's entire life.

At home, Carli skipped into their shared house, her high heels providing no barrier to the speed with which they rushed inside. and as soon as the front door closed, the stripping started. James tore off his shirt, not caring that he ripped off buttons. Carli kicked off her heels, but she remained standing on her toes, her calves too tight to let her heels touch the ground.

Their clothes came off as they made their way to the bedroom, deposited wherever they fell. As soon as they reached the bedroom, James pulled Carli into a tight embrace, kissing her hard on the lips. Her big tits pressed into his torso as his hard cock pressed against her. Their mouths parted for a moment and Carli moaned in appreciation. The new voice in her head had given her a lust for this man that had been long since dormant.

"I love you," James said. He felt like the luckiest guy in the world, dating such a beautiful and sexy girl. Carla had been more than a girlfriend when it came to sex, but now there was no question. This was his woman and he intended to do anything possible to make her happy.

"I love you, too," Carli said back, a smile coming to her lips as she let loose another giggle. It was easy to show the affection between them. All that really mattered were their hearts and what was inside of them. Nothing could stop them from loving each other.

With one hand on Carli's ass and the other still locked with hers, James began guiding her towards the bed. He set her down gently, pushing her up the bed until her head rested on the pillow. She watched him over her big tits, unable to see her body below them.

But Carli did not need to see when she could feel instead. James parted her legs and leaned down until his lips hovered tantalizingly close to her pussy. He had always wanted to do this, to pleasure his girlfriend with his mouth, but Carla had always stopped him. But it was now Carli in charge and James was confident she would enjoy herself.

"I'm going to eat your pussy," James announced, but he did not wait for Carli to respond. He dove in, taking a full lick along her lower lips.

"Yes," Carli moaned as she reached out and ran her hands through her boyfriend's red hair. His tongue teased the entrance of her pussy before he dove deep, slurping up her juices. But there was no way she could last for more than a minute, such was her arousal. She came hard, squirting onto his tongue, coating it completely. The taste of her made him want to keep going, but it was not long before the orgasm faded, replaced by an insatiable desire.

Carli felt like the sexiest woman on earth. It was amazing how much the transformation had altered her personality, not that the old Carla ever felt all that sexy. Now Carli knew how to enjoy sex, especially with her boyfriend. He gave her exactly what she needed. And what she needed now was cock.

James pulled back for a moment to breathe and he glanced up at Carli, his eyes roaming over her body, taking in every detail of the naked girl before him. She had never looked so good, with her big tits bouncing gently as she arched her back. There was no hint of sag. They were firm and stood up from her chest, even when she was on her back.

"Please, fuck me," Carli moaned as her fingers ran across her taut midriff to the junction between her thighs. She had already cum once, and all too quickly, but she was a slut for more, needing to not just cum, but to orgasm on the big cock of James. She would not let him go without giving her everything.

"What did you say?" James asked, still staring at his girlfriend, her face red and sweaty with pleasure, a sly smile on his face. Her nipples were so hard they stuck straight out. Her whole body was ripe with desire and lust. There was not a man alive who could deny her his cock, but she was all his.

"I want your cock so bad," Carli said breathily.

"I like it when you beg," James told her as he positioned himself at her entrance. His cock pressed into her wet pussy and she gasped out loud. She was tight, her pussy perfectly formed for his cock. He pushed forward slowly and Carli groaned as he went deeper inside of her. Her hands gripped the bed sheets beneath her, almost ripping holes in them with her long nails.

"Oh god yes," Carli panted, not even sure what she was saying, her words becoming less coherent by the second. She had never felt this way before. So much of her life had simplified as she became Carli, but a whole new world of sex and pleasure had been opened up to her, more than making up for any loss she might have experienced. It was all she could do to not start cumming again. She had never felt so turned on. She could barely breathe.

"Please fuck me, please fuck my brains out, oh god," Carli cried out as a second orgasm hit her, this one stronger than before, gushing all over her boyfriend's cock. And yet, despite two orgasms, Carli was not even close to being done, to being satisfied. She needed more. She wanted him to fuck her so hard she would never walk or talk ever again, at least metaphorically. She would become one with his cock and be completely devoted to the only man she loved.

"You don't know how many times I came to this fantasy," James said, thinking back to those lonely nights spent alone, needing to use his hands to find pleasure and relief, imagining his girlfriend had turned into some semblance of a bimbo. And now she had transformed, just like Beth and Bekki, becoming a hot, blonde bimbo in her own right. She had changed so much and still James loved every moment of it. He would give anything to make her happy. He already knew she made him happy, no matter what happened next.

But James was still pumping into her, driving his cock in and out of her tight pussy, her muscles bearing down on him, trying to milk his cock for all it was worth. The way her eyes rolled into the back of her head made him know that she was about to come again.

And she did, again, harder than ever before, squirting

onto the sheets beneath them. But that was enough to push him over the edge. They came together, his cock surging with cum, filling as she thrashed beneath him in orgasmic convulsions. His cock pulsed and shot rope after rope into the beautiful bimbo beneath him, her big tits heaving with the force of his thrusts.

Afterward, the two lay there, catching their breath, James still buried deep inside his girlfriend, unable to pull out just yet. He wanted to stay inside her forever, but they had not finished their date night just yet. He pulled his softening cock from her wet pussy, watching as he came out from her entrance.

"You are so beautiful, Carli," James said as he looked over her body, taking in every inch, her perfect breasts, the cute little belly button and flat tummy, even her pretty face. Carli did not respond. Instead, she just lay there, panting. She knew that her boyfriend would do anything for her, that she was his world and he would die to make sure she was happy. And she knew it was true in reverse. She would do anything he asked of her without a second thought. Hers was not to question, but to act, to arouse, to fuck. Those were her strongest desires, having become a devoted bimbo for her boyfriend.

But the night was not over yet. It was still early and Carli still had work to do. She needed to make sure James came again and a gain, using her body to get him off as much as possible. He had used her pussy, but there was so much more to her than just a pussy. She had a mouth, ass, hands, and even her two tits to make sure he got off, using her slutty body to fulfill his every desire.

Carli jumped into action, turning her body so that she was on her hands and knees. She lowered her lips and kissed the tip of James' cock. He moaned as the tip slipped past her lips, maintaining a tight 'O' shape around his shaft. She slowly took more and more of him inside, his cock growing hard again as she went, working her way down his shaft with each passing moment. By the time her mouth reached his balls, he was buried deep in her throat, without any hint of a gag reflex.

"Holy shit," James gasped. He could not believe how quickly she had gotten him hard again after cumming only minutes before. He was so amazed at what she had unleashed that he was willing to try just about anything. And there was no man who could complain about his sexy girlfriend going down on him, using just her mouth to get him hard again.

Carli purred, the vibrations in her throat adding to James' pleasure. She was in heaven, loving every moment. It did not matter that her air supply was cut off while she had his cock in her throat. She would come up for air when it was needed. She wanted to maximize his pleasure. And did it matter if she burned off another couple brain cells along the way. Even she would admit she did not need them anymore. As long as she had access to her boyfriend's cock, she was a happy bimbo.

"I'm going to cum," James announced. There was no point in trying to hold back any longer. Carli had done so well already. She had him ready to blow again and he wanted to know how Carli would react.

She pulled back, just enough to keep the head of his cock in her mouth. She wrapped her fingers around his shaft, jacking him while she prepared to receive his seed.

James let loose a surge of hot, white cum into her mouth. He groaned as it erupted from his balls, coating the inside of her cheeks, hitting the back of her tongue with each shot, and sliding down her throat. It tasted better than anything she ever had before. It was sweet ambrosia, almost heady enough to make her drunk. She would have giggled at the idea of her being a cum drunk bimbo, but her mouth was still occupied by the cock in her mouth.

She kept milking his cock for every last drop, swallowing what she could as quickly as possible. James had cum so much already, but she was a selfish cum addict. She needed it all.

Carli licked and sucked every bit of cum off of her boyfriend, taking his seed into her belly so that it was not wasted.

"Damn, that was good," James said as he slapped her ass. He loved everything about his bimbo girlfriend.

"Mmm," Carli moaned. "Do that again. Slap my bubble butt."

She waved her ass toward James and waited for his open palm to hit her again. She moaned upon contact, loving the surge of arousal she received from the rough treatment.

James pulled her up next to him. She laid out on her side, pressing her tits into his arm. She leaned forward and pressed her plump lips to his. James kissed back, running his fingers through her hair behind her head and pulling her in, crushing her into him.

"Oh god, Carli, you feel amazing," James groaned as he felt how soft her skin was against him. She smelled of a new perfume, something flowery with a hint of jasmine. But then he realized it wasn't perfume. It was her new smell of sex. And that made him hard all over again. His dick stood at attention as he went back to kissing his beautiful and sexy bimbo girlfriend.

Carli knew what was coming next. She wanted him inside her again. He had been inside her already, but that didn't stop her from wanting more.

"Fuck my ass," Carli begged as soon as they came up for air. "Please."

James smiled down at her. He loved this part. He had

always wanted to try anal, but Carla had been adamantly against it. But Carli had transformed into not just a bimbo, but a complete slut as well. Her brain was no longer the center of her existence. Instead, it was the pleasure her body generated through the act of sex.

"As you wish, my bimbo," James said as he climbed to his knees. He pushed Carli's legs up to her head, taking advantage of her newfound flexibility, forcing her impressive ass up as well.

Carli giggled and cooed as he prepared himself. He dipped his fingers into her still sopping wet pussy, gathering her fluids. He rubbed them all over his cock. Then he went back for more to prepare her ass, using her own juices as lubrication. She moaned in anticipation.

"Stick it in me," Carla said as she wiggled her ass up and down in response to her boyfriend preparing her hole. It was time. Time for the main event. And there was nothing better than the moment when her boyfriend slid into her tight little asshole.

James groaned as his cock sank deep into her tight butt. Carli gasped, loving how good it felt. There was little she could do, folded in half as she was. But the pleasure was still intense, easily overriding any pain that came with such a dirty act.

"Oh yeah, Carli, take my cock," James gasped. "I want to feel your tight ass around my cock."

He pumped his hips forward, driving his cock deeper inside her tight rectum. The tip bumped against the deepest reaches of her body, sending a tingling sensation through her body.

Carla cooed in delight. The sensation of James' cock being so far inside her now made her giddy. She wanted more. More. MORE!

"Oh yes," James panted. "You're such a perfect slut, my bimbo. Do you want to cum?"

He pulled back and pushed back in. His cock glided along the walls of her anal canal. Each time he drove inside, a new wave of pleasure coursed through her body. He knew she did not have much brain power left, but still he teased her, knowing the only thing that could make her happy would be another orgasm.

"Yes," she whimpered. "Please. Make me cum again. I love your cock so much!"

He pulled back, letting his cock pop out of her butt for just a second before slamming it back in. This time she moaned in response. Her body writhed on the bed as the wave of pleasure swept over her.

"Fuck my ass, babe," Carli whispered as she lay beneath her boyfriend, trying to catch her breath. He was so hard. So big and long.

James groaned at the feel of his cock buried balls deep in Carli's asshole. He had taken the bimbo up every hole now. But there was something about having the tightest asshole around take him in and milk him while he fucked her behind. It was new and exotic and he loved it, just as much as she did.

"Are you ready for more, little bimbo slut?" James asked. "I'm going to make you cum again."

Carli wiggled her ass, wanting to get him inside her even harder this time.

"That's right, my little anal whore," James growled in reply. "Take my cock in that beautiful ass of yours."

He pumped his hips, fucking his cock back into her asshole. This time it took a lot less effort to drive his shaft into her. He was lasting longer this time, having cum so much already, but even he was human. He was so close.

"Cum on my cock, bimbo," he grunted as he felt his

orgasm approaching. His cock filled with warm, milky cream.

And then it exploded out of him, filling her bowels. And Carli was cumming, too, her body shaking as another orgasm cascaded through her body.

Carli lay on the bed in ecstasy, her asshole spasming in reaction to James' powerful orgasm making her cum as well. She had never come so hard before. It was almost like she was possessed by some unknown force of lust, a bimbo goddess of surreal sexual powers. The feeling made her shiver uncontrollably, her body just about reaching its limit. Her last bit of pleasure came from the sensation of James pulling out of her ass.

"Oh god, baby, I love your cock so much," Carli whispered between her moans as she felt her asshole tighten around James' cum. He let her legs back down, allowing her to relax. She was almost delirious after all those orgasms. "It feels so good inside me. It makes me so wet. You're amazing. Amazing!"

She giggled and moaned as she fell into a blissful sleep.

James got up from the bed and walked into the bathroom. A quick shower to clean himself was all he would need before a potential new round. Before climbing into the shower, James looked in the mirror and smiled. This bimbo girlfriend of his was really something else. He had always thought she was hot, but now she was a bimbo, completely devoted to him. And when that bimbo woke up? Oh god. It was going to be even hotter. He turned on the water and got ready for round two.

The shower was still running when Carli woke up from her nap. She hugged her body, pushing her big tits up toward her chin. They were soft and pliant, yet firm and buoyant, with their big nipples standing at attention. She could not remember how many orgasms she had enjoyed. But she did know that they had all been mind-blowing. The pleasure had been too intense to count. It was like some kind of orgasmic nirvana. And this new side of herself wanted to keep having more orgasms.

"Wow," Carli murmured to herself, remembering what had just happened. It was all so amazing. She had a wonderful boyfriend who would keep her well-fucked. Nothing else mattered.

Carli climbed up off the bed and tip-toed toward the closet. She was not sure what she would find. A part of her new she had once been boring and unsexy. Would she need to go shopping for a new wardrobe? As a bimbo, she wasn't against that, but it was a lot of work.

Opening the door, Carli was greeted by bright and skimpy clothing, short dresses and skirts, plunging necklines and enough shoes to never wear the same pair more than once per month. She squealed in delight at seeing all the pretty colors. The magic from the Bimbo Wine had not just transformed her body and mind, but her whole life.

There was no doubt in Carli's mind that she was better off as a bimbo. She was so happy, she did not even know how to be sad. And she could not wait to meet up with her bimbofied friends and their boyfriends. Carli, Beth, and Bekki were going to make a great team. And the orgy potential boggled her bimbofied mind.

However, there was one thing left that she still wanted to do. Leaving the closet behind, Carli swayed into the bathroom. James was still in the shower, lightly humming to himself. She giggled before she moved to join him, wanting to fuck him with her tits. Once they had done so, there was no way anyone could argue she was not his bimbo. And that all Carli wanted anymore, to belong to her boyfriend. And it was all thanks to Bimbo Wine.

ABOUT THE AUTHOR

Sadie Thatcher is a longtime author of erotic fiction, especially related to transformations and bimbofication. She likes to say "I have thrown off the shackles of my conservative upbringing and now write erotic stories."

She maintains several blogs devoted to her writings, including a behind the scenes look at her writing process, and bimbos in general, as well as highlights works by other authors. They can be found at:

https://authorsadiethatcher.tumblr.com

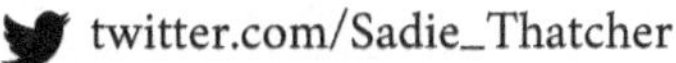 twitter.com/Sadie_Thatcher

The Curse of Playing Bimbo Tag

The Curse of Playing Bimbo Tag: Jenna or Jenni

The Bimbo Professor: The Curse of Playing Bimbo Tag Book 3

Anything for the Job

Anything for the Job 2

Anything for His Job

The Bimbo in the Mirror

The Bimbo in the Mirror 2

Astrid and the Bimbo Bee

Bella and the Bimbo Bee

Cali and the Bimbo Bee

Desiree and the Bimbo Bee

Ember and the Bimbo Bee

Fiona and the Bimbo Bee

The Intern

The Lawyer

The Hacker

Cause & Effect

Witless Protection

Stealing Sally

Trial and Error

Beta Testing

Exposed

Bimbo for a Weekend

Bimbo for a Week

Bimbo for Life

Surprise!

Best Laid Plans

No Going Back

Bigger

Fake It Until You Make It Season 1

Fake It Until You Make It Season 2

Fake It Until You Make It Season 3

Fake It Until You Make It Season 4

Fake It Until You Make It Season 5

Fake It Until You Make It Season 6

Simple and Fun Volume 1

Simple and Fun Volume 2

Simple and Fun Volume 3

Simple and Fun Volume 4

Simple and Fun Volume 5

Simple and Fun Volume 6

Silly Bimbo Volume 1

Silly Bimbo Volume 2

Silly Bimbo Volume 3

Bimbo Halloween

Bimbo Christmas

Bimbo Technology

Dorm Room Bimbo

Carissa's Magic Pen

Spirit Walk

Muscle Memory

The Case of the Bimbo Wife

Changes

Changes 2

New Year New You

Bigfoot and the Bimbo

Bimbo Zero

Going Native

Thanks for Giving

Working for Bimbo Claus

The Spirit of Bimbo Christmas

The Bimbo Sweater

What Really Happened to D.B. Cooper

Starting Over

Milk and Bliss

The Fighter

The Help

The Bimbo Resort

Awakening

Bubblegum and Latex

Vanity

Christmas Wish

Body Swap Rings: Happy Anniversary

Body Swap Rings 2: Wedding Night

The Bimbo Experience

The Bimbo Experience 2

The Bimbo Experience 3some

The 4th Bimbo Experience

Bimbo Genes

Bimbo Genes II: The Virus

The Bimbo Genes III: The Epidemic

Bimbo Juice: Blue Raspberry

Bimbo Juice: Grape

Bimbo Juice: Mango

Bimbo Juice: Pineapple

Bimbo Juice: Red Apple

Bimbo Juice: Veggie

Bimbo Juice Gone Wild: The Muse

Bimbo Juice Gone Wild: Street Racer

Bimbo Juice Gone Wild: Score

Bimbos of the Traveling Earrings: Book 1

Bimbos of the Traveling Earrings: Book 2

Bimbos of the Traveling Earrings: Book 3

Bimbos of the Traveling Earrings: Book 4

Bimbo Party: Kennedy

Bimbo Party: Esme

Bimbo Party: Ariana

Bimbo Party: Tara

Workout Buddies

Wishful Thinking

Wanting More

Bimbo Harem: Annabelle

Bimbo Harem: Josie

Bimbo Harem: Nikki

Bimbo Harem: Tiana

Giggle Dust

Giggle Dust 2.0

Giggle Dust 3.0

Giggle Dust 4.0

Bimbo Takeover: The First Step

Bimbo Takeover: Teammates

Joining Bimbodom

Bimbo Salon

Bimbo Vision

Spiral

Rerun

Housemates

One of Us

Inevitable

Life in Plastic

Plastic Guilt

Plastic Fantastic

Leadership

Founders

Hostile Takeover

Cheers

Happy Hour

Date Night